Eternal Love

NASU

Published by MOHAMMED KAIF, 2024.

ETERNAL LOVE

First edition. July 19, 2024.

Copyright © 2024 NASU.

ISBN: 979-8227669155

Written by NASU.

ABOUT THE AUTHOR:

Mr. M. Kaif

Mohammed Kaif, a 20-year-old student from India, is a burgeoning author with an unyielding passion for storytelling. Currently pursuing his engineering degree at PES University, Bangalore, M. Kaif has dedicated his academic journey to honing his writing skills and exploring the vast world of literature.

From an early age, M. Kaif discovered his love for stories of all kinds. Whether it was fantasy, mystery, romance, or adventure, he found joy in weaving intricate tales that captivate and inspire. His ability to craft compelling narratives has not only been a personal passion but also a driving force behind his academic pursuits.

As a young writer, M. Kaif brings a fresh and unique perspective to the literary world. His imaginative mind and creative flair allow him to create stories that resonate with readers of all ages. Each title he chooses to write is a journey in itself, filled with rich characters, vivid settings, and thought-provoking plots.

In his second book, "Eternal Love," M. Kaif invites readers to join him on a literary adventure that promises to be both engaging and unforgettable. His dedication to his craft and his ability to evoke emotion through his words make him a promising new voice in contemporary literature.

M. Kaif's enthusiasm for writing is evident in every page of his work. His commitment to storytelling and his passion for creating memorable narratives are sure to make a lasting impact on the literary community. With "Eternal Love," M. Kaif continues his journey in the world of published authors, ready to share his stories with the world and leave an indelible mark on his readers.

Prepare to be transported into the captivating worlds created by M. Kaif, a talented young author whose journey is just beginning. "Eternal Love" is a testament to his skill and creativity, and it is only the second of many stories he has yet to share.

"Dream big, only if you are capable of completing your smaller dreams."

CONTENT

The   Mysterious   Egg

In a village named Frank wood, far from the bustling city of Silver City, there was a secretive research centre. This centre was deeply hidden in the dense forest surrounding the village, and its focus was on a colossal egg. The egg had been discovered at the bottom of a deep ocean trench, where it had remained undisturbed for countless years. Standing at about four feet tall, the egg was unearthed and brought to the research centre through immense effort and numerous challenges.

However, the research on the egg was conducted without the government's approval. A group of scientists, driven by their curiosity, had set up the research centre illegally, far from the city to avoid detection. After extensive investigations, they discovered that the egg belonged to a creature never before seen by humanity—only imagined in myths and movies. The egg's unique shell could absorb the surrounding temperature, remaining liquid inside the water but solid outside on land, preventing it from decomposing in the ocean depths.

Despite their groundbreaking findings, an unfortunate accident occurred at the research centre, alerting the government to their unauthorized activities. In response, the government swiftly sealed the centre and arrested all the scientists involved, revoking their licenses and suspending them indefinitely. Before the centre was sealed, the scientists managed to hide the egg in the basement, a secret known only to them.

Two Years Later

Central College

In Silver City, there was a college named Silver Central College where Kevin, a seemingly ordinary student, stood out. He was quiet, rarely spoke to anyone, and always dressed modestly in plain clothes. Despite his reserved nature, Kevin consistently ranked among the top two students academically. Hailing from a middle-class background, he carried himself with simplicity and humility.

Kevin was part of a close-knit friend group comprising four boys—himself, Alex, Ben, and David—and three girls—Kara, Lily, and Bella.

Beauty in Wealth

Kara was the daughter of a wealthy family, with a very affluent background. She was a very beautiful girl with a bob haircut. She had fair skin with a light complexion and was often described as having a natural and classic beauty. Her eyes were brown and beautiful, adding a unique sparkle to her face.

Echoes of Silence

In the class, Kara was universally liked, and she served as the leader of the group of seven. Alex, who was Kara's boyfriend, was also wealthy, being the son of Kara's father's boss. Ben was Alex's best friend, and Lily was his companion. David and Bella, like Alex and Kara, were also a couple.

Kevin was the odd one out in the group, but he and Kara were the top two achievers among them. Kevin was highly intelligent and had a deep love for poetry, particularly admiring the works of William Shakespeare. His dream was to pursue poetry, and he had a talent for turning everyday words and sentences into poetic expressions. Despite his intellectual interests, Kevin didn't come from a wealthy background like the others. He was careful with his spending, focusing more on saving money. Kevin always maintained a calm demeanour.

Whispers of Love

Kevin wrote all his poems in Kara's name, deeply inspired by her, though no one knew that Kevin's poems were dedicated to her. He loved Kara immensely and cared deeply for her, but Kara never understood Kevin's feelings beyond seeing him as a competitive partner, especially since they both often ranked in the top two. Sometimes Kara would come first, and sometimes Kevin would.

Echoes of Struggle

Kevin lived ten kilometres away from his college and would commute there by bicycle or bus, unlike his friends who arrived in cars. Throughout college, Kevin endured constant teasing and insults from others, who mocked him for being from a poor family, calling him names like "idiot from a poor background." Despite consistently achieving top grades, Kevin received little respect or recognition. Most people ignored him, and even Kara only spoke to him when she needed help with academic questions, which Kevin gladly answered.

Whenever Kevin saw Kara with Alex, he felt deeply saddened and would distract himself by reading books by William Shakespeare in frustration.

David's Support

Kevin had a good friend named David, who not only was his bench mate but also happened to be the owner of the house where Kevin lived. They had been schoolmates, which strengthened their bond even further. David had always been very supportive of Kevin, often helping him out whenever he could.

David's Generosity

When Kevin's father faced significant losses in his business, resulting in financial strain where they couldn't afford rent, David stepped in to help. Knowing Kevin and his family from school and being Kevin's bench mate, David offered them his old house, located far away, for them to live in. He assured them not to worry about rent until they were financially stable again, saying, "Pay me back whenever you can."

This act of kindness meant a lot to Kevin's family, who were overjoyed and relieved by David's support. David, having lost his own parents in a car accident, lived with his grandmother. He managed his late father's estate, which included several valuable assets. After the accident, David had moved to a new house near the college, keeping his father's legacy safe.

Bella's Rescue

When David found himself entirely alone in life, and Kevin's family was also facing financial troubles due to his father's failing business, Kevin withdrew and didn't talk to David as much. At this time, David had moved to a new house near the college, where his neighbour Bella lived.

One day, in a moment of deep depression over his parents' death, David attempted suicide by standing in front of a fast-moving car on the road outside his house. Bella intervened just in time, pulling him back and telling him to open his eyes to the road. David replied with anguish, "I can see the road, I can see the car, I can see the world, but I can't see my parents."

Understanding his intent, Bella comforted him with the words, "Good things can't be seen through the eyes, but they can be felt through the heart." These words resonated deeply with David, and he appreciated Bella's insight. When they introduced themselves to each other, David realized Bella was his neighbour. Grateful for her timely intervention, David invited Bella into his home, where they found solace in each other's company.

As they walked home together, stopping at a shop for ice cream and chatting along the way, David and Bella formed a bond that helped David heal and begin to embrace life again. Learning about Kevin's family's financial struggles and his father's business problems, David immediately stepped in to help. Bella also decided to join David's college and ended up in the same class, further cementing their friendship.

Ben's Nocturnal Drive

Ben also lived in Silver City and worked as a part-time taxi driver during nighttime. Despite being the son of the taxi company owner, Ben preferred to keep his identity hidden. He enjoyed driving immensely, which led him to take on this job secretly. If anyone discovered that Ben was the owner's son, they would refuse to let him drive, so he operated secretly, starting his shifts stealthily from home.

Rescued by Chance

One night, Ben drove a passenger to a grand mansion adorned for an upcoming wedding. As Ben prepared to leave after dropping off his customer, a beautiful, well-dressed young woman hailed his taxi. She concealed her face and insisted Ben drive away quickly from the mansion. Ben understood she was fleeing from there and drove away swiftly.

When Ben asked where she wanted to go, the woman revealed herself as Lily. She explained that she had fled her wedding because it was forced upon her to a wealthy man named Kim, whom she didn't love. Learning about her situation, Ben lightened the mood with a funny line: "Where there is a will, there is a way. If there is no will, there is still a way and that is to run!" Lily smiled through her distress, and Ben immediately earned her trust.

Ben hid Lily in his old farmhouse. Over time, Lily's parents realized their mistake in pressuring her into the marriage with Kim, who turned out to be a bad person. They returned the money and broke off the alliance, regretting their actions. Lily's father, deeply remorseful, sat by the sea in despair, where Ben found him. Lily had already told Ben about her father's greed but insisted he was not a bad person. Ben convinced Lily's father to visit the farmhouse, where Lily embraced her parents, and they apologized to her.

Bonds Beyond Grades

In their first year of college, Kevin consistently topped the class while Kara closely followed. By the second year, Kevin, Kara, David, Ben, Bella, Lily, and Alex had all become close friends, forming a tight-knit group. Kevin remained intelligent and reserved, Kara assertive, David friendly, Alex affluent, Bella nurturing, and Lily sensitive to even the smallest slights.

Their diverse personalities and shared experiences bound them together beyond academic achievements, shaping their college journey with camaraderie and support.

The Bonds of Support

During their first-year semester exams, the seven friends found themselves seated in the same row. Alex and Ben struggled with a particularly tough question that was compulsory to attempt, without which they risked failing. Alex, seated next to a student named Ben who was facing the same dilemma, turned to him for help. Despite both needing to pass, neither knew the answer.

When neither knew the answer, Alex turned to Kevin for help, but Kevin remained silent, preferring to keep to himself except for interactions with David. Kara, determined to maintain her academic standing, chose not to assist Alex, concerned that helping him might affect her own performance.

Feeling that Kara might not have heard him or chose to ignore his request, Alex then directly asked Ben for help. Ben, aware of Kevin's reluctance to interact with others, sought David's assistance, knowing David was his cousin and Kevin's close friend So, when Alex asked David for help, David then asked Ben to get the answer from Kevin, and when Kevin gave the answer to David, it reached Ben and Alex.

Friendship and Forgiveness

After the exam, Kevin apologized to Ben for not providing the answer because he was focused on solving the next question and couldn't interrupt his concentration. When Ben asked during the same question, Kevin couldn't provide the answer to the previous question. Then Alex and Ben said, "No worries, we got the answer. David had told us." When Alex asked Kevin how he gave the answer to David, Ben replied that when David asked, he had already solved the other question and was free, so he could provide the answer. This reason was understood.

Introductions and Unspoken Feelings

When Alex and Ben introduced themselves, they also introduced Kevin and David. David, already acquainted with Bella through Kevin, had previously heard about her from David. Now, Alex and Ben introduced Kara and Lily to David and Kevin. However, Kevin was already familiar with Kara because he had been admiring her since their college days, finding happiness in seeing her every day. However, Kara did not reciprocate Kevin's feelings at all.

Deceptive Intentions

Alex's father was Kara's father's boss, which led to their introduction. They decided to collaborate on managing their respective businesses in the future. Alex, known for his wealth and good looks, regularly flaunted his affluence by purchasing expensive items and showering Kara with gifts. He strategically courted Kara due to her family's substantial wealth, intending to marry her to gain control of her future inheritance. His plan was to divorce her after securing her assets. Despite appearing kind and generous publicly, Alex concealed a manipulative and malicious nature. Kara, unaware of Alex's true intentions, remained charmed by his facade.

The Magnificent Seven

In the first-year exams, Kevin topped the class, which made Kara increasingly jealous of him. In the next semester, all the friends—Kevin, Kara, David, Ben, Lily, Alex, and Bella—found themselves in the same class. They formed a close-knit group and named themselves "The Magnificent Seven."

In this group of seven friends, strong bonds of friendship formed among them. However, Kevin was not liked by Alex and Kara. To them, Kevin was just a poor boy. Kara befriended Kevin solely for her own benefit, aiming to defeat him in the semester and secure the top position for herself.

Alex's Secret Discovery

One day, Alex secretly checks Kevin's personal diary from his bag. He is shocked to find Kara's name written in it, filled with numerous poems expressing Kevin's love for her. Angered by this discovery, Alex knows he can't tell anyone, as it would expose his own plans. He carefully places the diary back as he found it. Now, Alex's hatred for Kevin deepens. Determined to ruin Kevin in Kara's eyes, he devises numerous plans with the help of his other group friends, secretly bribing them to assist in his schemes.

The next day, when "The Magnificent Seven" arrived at college, they found posters plastered everywhere about Kevin. The posters claimed that Kevin's father was involved in illegal activities to grow his business and that Kevin helped him. It also said that when the police found out, Kevin's father was jailed and kicked out of the business. After being released from jail, Kevin's father allegedly took over David's house. This rumour quickly spread throughout the college.

Kevin feels deeply hurt upon seeing the false story on the posters, but Alex is secretly delighted because it was his plan all along. When Kara starts to mock Kevin after seeing the posters, David and Bella immediately come to Kevin's defence. They explain to everyone that the posters are lies and start removing them. Kevin appreciates David and Bella's support immensely, and he begins to feel a little better amidst the situation.

Alex's Devious Plan-1

Next day, Alex devises another plan to undermine Kevin in Kara's eyes. When everyone went for lunch at the college canteen, they brought their food to the dining tables and sat down. Alex asked Kevin if he could pass his plate, saying he'd accidentally left it behind. Kevin agreed and got up to retrieve it. The plate was full of food, and as Kevin approached to hand it over, Alex stuck out his foot and nudged the plate towards where Kara was sitting. The plate toppled over Kara, spilling food all over her.

Kara got very angry and when Alex tried to explain, she wouldn't listen. She thought Kevin did it intentionally, and in her anger, she slapped him hard across the face. When David, Bella, Ben, Lily, and the rest of the students saw this, they were shocked. The other students in the college started making fun of Kevin, laughing at his humiliation. Kevin started feeling very embarrassed, tears welling up in his eyes. He tried to hold it in but couldn't. Kara stormed off after slapping Kevin, leaving him standing there, ashamed and teary-eyed. He eventually ran away from there, far from the college, to the seashore, where he sat under a tree and cried a lot. He had never felt so humiliated before. He kept blaming himself, wondering what he had done wrong. He kept saying to himself, 'Why did she do that to me? I didn't do anything wrong. I really liked her.' He kept talking to himself and crying.

David and Bella Comfort Kevin

David and Bella arrived and saw Kevin crying. They went to console him. David said, "It's not your fault. I saw Alex deliberately trip you. I saw everything and was about to tell Kara, but it all happened so quickly. Please forgive me, my friend. Don't be sad. Bella and I are here for you."

Kevin then showed them his diary, revealing his deep love for Kara. He told them about the beautiful lines he had written for her. David and Bella were shocked and asked why he hadn't told Kara about his feelings. Kevin replied, Kara likes Alex. I don't want to take her happiness away. Seeing her happy with Alex makes me happy too.

He then made David and Bella promise not to tell anyone about his feelings, especially Kara. He didn't want anyone to know. David replied, "Kara doesn't deserve to know. She doesn't deserve your love."

Kevin said, "It's not Kara's fault. She only reacted to what she saw. She didn't know what actually happened, so she can't be blamed." Hearing this, David and Bella looked at each other, realizing how good-hearted Kevin was. Despite everything, he still spoke in defence of Kara.

David and Bella's friendship with Kevin grew even deeper. The three of them returned to college together, their bond stronger than ever. Seeing them together made Alex even angrier, and he started thinking of a new plan.

As the second-year exams were approaching, everyone became busy with their preparations. However, Alex was plotting something new.

Alex's Devious Plan-2

Everyone was busy preparing for the upcoming exams. However, Alex had devised a new scheme to ensure he passed the exams and further tarnished Kevin's image in Kara's eyes. This time, Alex bribed the college principal with a significant amount of money to get the exam papers. The principal accepted the bribe and handed over the exam papers to Alex.

Alex wrote all the exams using the leaked papers. On the last day of the exams, Alex hurriedly wrote his paper and then discreetly placed the leaked exam papers into Kevin's bag, ensuring no one noticed. His plan was to make it look like Kevin had cheated, hoping this would ruin Kevin's reputation even further.

After the exams were over, everyone was called to the class to discuss the next semester. As everyone gathered, they began asking each other how their exams went, with many agreeing that the papers were quite tough.

In the meantime, Alex quietly told one of his friends from another group about his scheme. He mentioned that he had seen the exam papers in Kevin's bag, implying that Kevin might have received the exam papers beforehand and cheated to get the top rank. Alex suggested that Kevin could be leaking the exam papers, spreading this rumour to tarnish Kevin's reputation further.

Alex's rumour quickly spread throughout the class. One of Alex's friends boldly checked Kevin's bag in front of everyone, pulling out the exam papers. The entire class was shocked, and their gazes turned accusatory towards Kevin. Kara, laughing at Kevin, mocked him, calling him the biggest coward and cheater, claiming that he must have cheated to come first in the first year. She insulted him further, saying he was worthless and illiterate, just like his father.

Kevin felt devastated hearing Kara's harsh words. The other students, fuelled by the rumour, started throwing pens, pencils, and rubbers at him, chanting "cheater, cheater." Amidst the chaos, Alex discreetly threw a stone at Kevin, hitting him hard and causing his head to bleed profusely.

Kevin's Rescue and Hospitalization

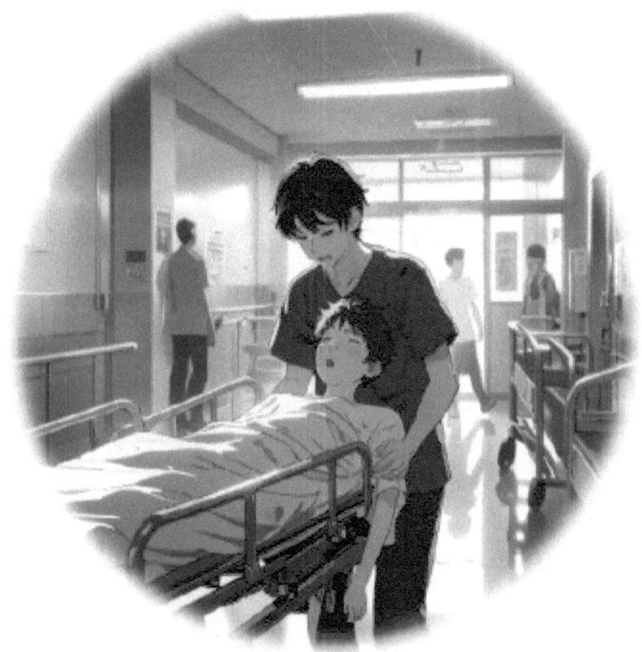

David and Bella, horrified by the scene, quickly rescued Kevin from the classroom and rushed him to the hospital. They managed to get him admitted to the emergency ward just in time. Their clothes were soaked with Kevin's blood.

A while later, the doctor came out and informed them that Kevin had lost a lot of blood. "If he had arrived any later, he might not have survived," but "We urgently need O-negative blood, but it's a rare type, and it's difficult to arrange in such a short time. We've also contacted his parents, but they are far away. Waiting for their blood might cost Kevin his life."

Bella quickly responded, "Please continue the treatment. My father has O-negative blood, and our house is nearby. He should be home now." She immediately called her father and arranged for him to come to the hospital with his blood donation.

Bella's father arrived promptly, and the blood was transfused to Kevin, ultimately saving his life.

A Life Saved

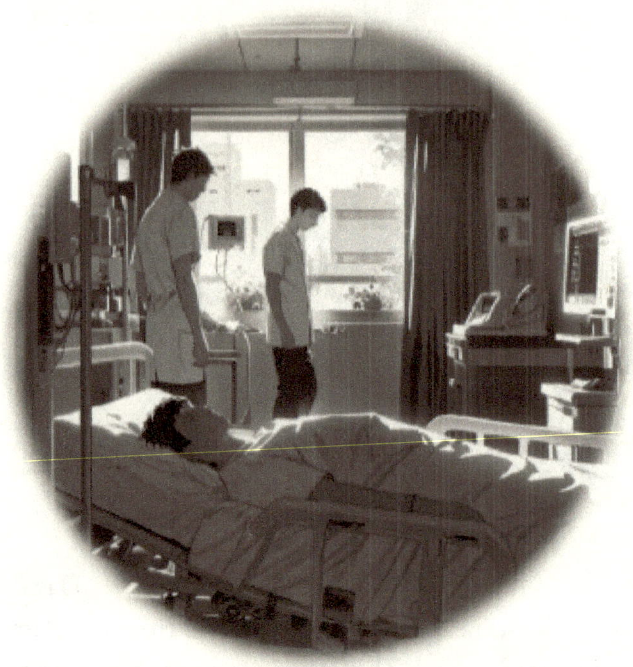

After some time, Kevin's parents arrived at the hospital, crying. David, Bella, and Bella's father comforted them, telling Kevin's parents not to worry. The doctor then said, "You should thank Bella's father. If he hadn't been here today, maybe your son wouldn't have survived." Kevin's parents expressed their gratitude to Bella's father, saying, "We had only one son. We had already lost one child, and if he had gone too, we wouldn't have been able to live." When Bella's father said, "There's no need to thank me. I am just happy that I could help someone."

Ben and Lily then arrived at the hospital to see Kevin. David and Bella felt very bad seeing Ben and Lily. They realized that Ben and Lily hadn't come to save Kevin. Everyone exchanged greetings and talked.

Ben then said to David, "Didn't you hear? There's a strike going on in our college. All the students are protesting against Kevin, and Alex is behind all of this. Alex told Kara that if Kevin is somehow expelled from college, she will top the college this year. Kara initially refused, but Alex convinced her and devised this plan, instigating all the students against Kevin. Everyone is saying Kevin should be investigated."

The news reached the chairman's office. With no other options, the chairman issued a letter to Kevin's parents about rustication him from the college for the leaked exam papers. the leaked exam papers. David and Bella were shocked to hear this. "Why would Alex do something so terrible to Kevin?" they wondered aloud.

David then informed Kevin's parents and Bella's father about the situation. Bella's father said, "You should file a case against the college for this. If your son didn't cheat, you should directly complain against the college. This is a matter of Kevin's life." David agreed, saying, "Yes, uncle and aunty, Kevin didn't leak any exam papers or cheat. He's a good boy." Bella also affirmed, "Kevin didn't cheat. I saw it myself. I went to borrow a pen from him before the exam, and those papers weren't in his bag."

Kevin's parents decided, "We'll go tomorrow morning and file a complaint against the college." Ben then relayed this news to Alex.

The Principal's Ultimatum

Ben then informed Alex about the plan to file a complaint. If a complaint were filed, both Alex and the principal would be caught. Alex rushed to the principal's office and requested the investigation be called off, promising to bring Kevin back to college. When the principal refused, Alex threatened, "If you don't comply, both of us will be caught." Fearing exposure, the principal immediately cancelled Kevin's expulsion with the chairman's permission and persuaded Kevin's parents not to file a complaint, saying, "Otherwise, our college's reputation will be tarnished." Reluctantly, Kevin's parents agreed.

Awakening

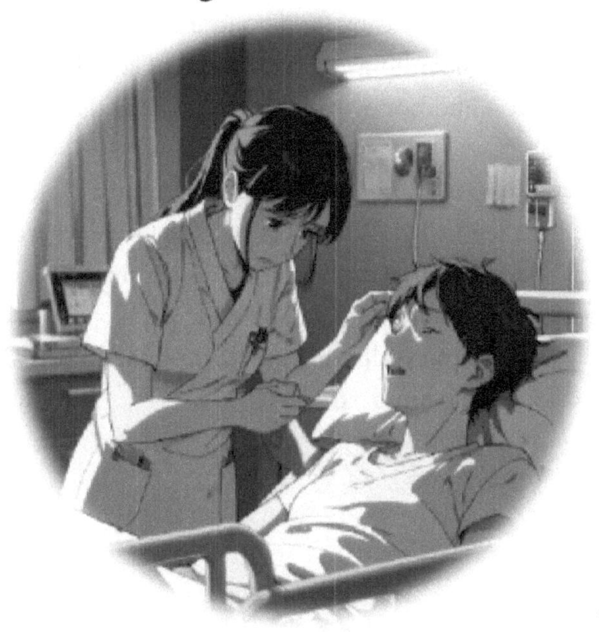

Ten days had passed, but Kevin still remained unconscious. Meanwhile, the college put up notices declaring Kevin innocent, stating he hadn't cheated and had been framed. Kara read all this and began feeling guilty. She went to the hospital that day with flowers for Kevin, apologizing and urging him to recover soon.

At that moment, Kevin slowly opened his eyes and saw Kara standing there. Overjoyed, he smiled. Kara immediately called the nurse, exclaiming that Kevin had regained consciousness. Kevin's parents rushed to his side, tears of joy filling their eyes. The nurse then asked everyone to step out for a while.

Road to Recovery

After some time, the doctor came and announced that Kevin was now stable and could be taken home in two to three days. He advised everyone to let Kevin rest and not disturb him too much, allowing only one visitor at a time.

One by one, everyone went to see Kevin. His mom went in first, followed by Bella, and then David. When Kevin asked David where Kara was, David replied, "Kara had to leave earlier for something urgent. But she brought a bouquet of flowers for you. She said, 'Be happy, Kevin,' as she left." David teased Kevin playfully, making Kevin smile a little. David then left Kevin's room, letting him rest.

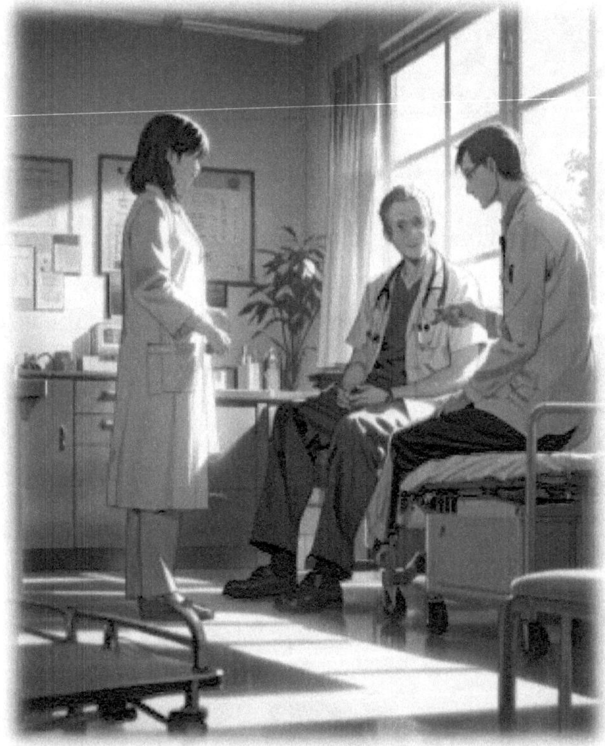

After three days, Kevin was cleared to leave the hospital. The doctor gave permission, and Kevin's parents, along with David and Bella, arrived with joyful expressions. Kevin's head was still bandaged, and David gently supported him, placing Kevin's arm around his shoulder and carefully guiding him into the car.

Before they left, the doctor instructed David, "Give him at least ten days of complete rest. Don't let him go anywhere, and if he experiences any headache, take him to the hospital immediately. Make sure he takes his medication on time."

Kara's Crisis

Kara was in tears when she received an urgent call at the hospital about her mother's accident and admission. Desperate to get to another hospital, she couldn't find a taxi. Kevin's father noticed her distress and asked, "What's wrong, dear? Why are you so upset? Is everything okay?"

Kara replied tearfully, "My mom had an accident. I need to get to the hospital, but I can't find a taxi." Hearing this, Kevin's father told David, "David, stay with Kevin. If there's an emergency, call me. I'll take Kara. I need Your Car, David agreed, "Sure, uncle," and handed over the car keys.

Kevin's father then took Kara to the other hospital. When they arrived, Kara's father still hadn't come. Upset and feeling abandoned, Kara called her father, who said he was too busy to come and asked her to manage. Kevin's father comforted Kara like a father would, helping her with her mother's medication, talking to the doctor, and reassuring her, "Trust in God. Everything will be okay." Kara felt comforted when the doctor later confirmed that her mother was out of danger.

When Kevin's father returned to the hospital after dropping Kara off, Kara began to feel remorseful. She started berating herself for saying hurtful things about Kevin's father in front of everyone at college. She cried, realizing how wrong she had been to speak ill of such a kind person.

Later, Kevin's father confided in David about Kara's situation. He explained that Kara's outburst stemmed from the stress of her mother's accident and hospitalization, and no one had been there to support her.

David shared this with Kevin after they returned from the hospital.

Kara's Gratitude

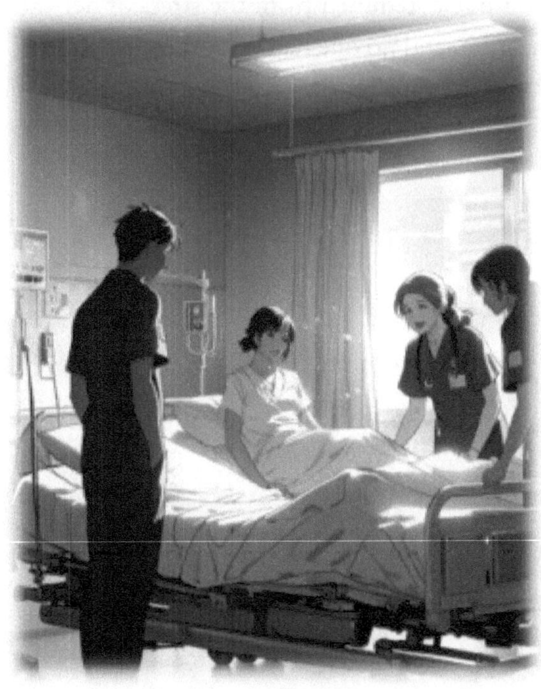

The next day, Kevin sent flowers to Kara's mother through his father and David, along with a letter expressing his apologies. The letter explained that the doctor had strictly instructed Kevin to stay home for ten days until he fully recovered, so he couldn't visit the hospital.

Upon reading the letter, Kara was touched and happy. David added, "Kevin was all set to come, but we convinced him not to because of his condition. You know how it is."

Kara agreed, "You did the right thing," and then Kevin's father asked, "How is your mother doing now?" Ben and Lily arrived to see her, and a while later, Kara's father arrived at the hospital.

Unpleasant Encounter

After Ben and Lily arrived and Kara's father finally showed up at the hospital, he insulted Kevin's father by saying, "What is this poor man doing in a rich hospital?" Kevin's father felt humiliated and quietly left the hospital with David. Kara couldn't muster the courage to speak up against her father's behaviour.

Reconciliation and Moving Forward

After ten days, Kevin returned to college with David and Bella. Kara also joined them, but she still harboured resentment towards Alex for not visiting the hospital, neither Kevin nor her mother. When Alex finally met Kara, he made excuses for not coming to the hospital, claiming he had gone to his village because his grandmother had passed away.

Upon hearing this, Kara was deeply hurt but reluctantly forgave him. Ben and Lily also arrived shortly after, asking about Kevin's well-being and Kara's mother. Kara assured them that her mother was doing well now.

Heartfelt Words

Kara felt deeply guilty upon seeing Kevin and apologized, asking for forgiveness for speaking ill of him and his father that day. Kevin responded tenderly:

"Don't make yourself hurt,

You are like a rose, piercing yet adored by all,

Thorns you may have, yet more beautiful than all.

A sight of you soothes the heart's pain,

Thorns forgotten, only your beauty remains.

Like a rose in bud, hiding before bloom,

You conceal your sadness, in silent gloom.

Seeing you, one wants to hide you away,

Like a cherished rose, unseen by day.

Beautiful you are, like a rose to all who see,

Your heart is a garden of roses to me.

When I see you, it's clear and true,

The most beautiful thing is your heart, and you."

Kara's heart filled with warmth upon hearing these beautiful lines. Even Lily and Bella admired Kevin's heartfelt words. However, Alex's mood darkened, sensing a shift in Kara's feelings towards Kevin.

The Unseen Answer

After the second-year exam results were announced, Kara unexpectedly secured the first position in college, while Kevin came in second. Everyone was shocked, including the professors, who urged Kevin to request a review of his paper. However, Kevin ignored their advice.

Taking matters into her own hands, Kara decided to review Kevin's paper herself. As she examined his answer sheet, she was astonished to find that Kevin had written "Dear Kara, you won" as the answer to the last question. This heartfelt gesture from Kevin had inadvertently cost him the first position and propelled Kara to the top.

Kara kept this discovery to herself, not showing Kevin's answer sheet to anyone. No one knew that Kara had reviewed Kevin's paper. Kevin's act of selflessness in allowing Kara to take the lead endeared him to Kara's heart. When Kevin later found his diary that he had accidentally left on his desk, Kara discovered it and realized her growing feelings for Kevin.

The Diary of Hearts

Kara took the diary back to her place and opened it. Tears streamed down her face as she found Kevin's diary filled with mentions of her name, woven into every story and poem. Each page resonated with his feelings for her. Kara felt herself drawn closer to Kevin, but she couldn't express it openly, especially with Alex still in the picture whom she liked.

Reading Kevin's diary made Kara feel more connected to him. She eventually handed the diary to Bella, who then gave it to David, with the intention that Kevin should not find out that Kara had read his diary. Kara didn't want Kevin to know because Kevin didn't want Kara to read it

Echoes of Remembrance

Late at night, Kara often found herself lost in memories of Kevin, recalling the poem he had publicly recited comparing her to a rose. She would reminisce about Kevin and express her feelings:

"If I am a rose, then you are my breeze,

Without you, my fragrance would not reach.
Without you, I wouldn't know who I am,
If I am the thorn, you are the stem.
With your support, I bloom with grace,
Hiding my silence, you embrace my pain.
I knew I was beautiful, but for you to see,
If I am the rose garden, you are the gardener for me.
You enhance my charm, make me complete,
If my heart is the most beautiful, you are its beat.
With you by my side, everything feels right,
Together, we shine, in day and night."

Between Hearts and Responsibilities

Kara feels more and more attached to Kevin, but remains silent because she is afraid of her father's reaction and doesn't want to betray Alex.

Police Investigation Clears Kevin

After the case reaches the police, it is revealed that the rumours about Kevin were false. Kevin is innocent, and someone had paid to spread these rumours. The police find out this information through an investigation led by Kara's uncle, who is very kind and dear to her. Kara talks to her uncle privately and explains the troubling incidents happening to Kevin since the first year. She requests him to find out who is behind this without informing her father. Her uncle agrees to investigate discreetly and promises to update her through a message or call.

As the third-year exams approach, everyone, including Kara and Kevin, becomes busy. Both Kara and Kevin excel in their exams, resulting in a tie for the top spot. Kara feels immense happiness, and Kevin does too. All the friends get promoted to their final year of graduation, marking the last year for the "Magnificent Seven."

Kevin's Poetry on Stage

In their final year, the college organizes numerous programs, including an event where Kara and Kevin are awarded certificates with scholarships. During the event, Kevin is asked to recite a poem on stage, as everyone knows he is good at it. Kara, standing among the students, also encourages him to recite a poem. Kevin, looking at Kara, begins his poetry:

"Standing before you, I introduce myself,
I am the star that shines, yet dims before your light.
You are the moon, serene and bright,
I am the sun that sets, you illuminate the night.

I am the warm breeze, you are the cool stream,
I am the sunbeam; you are the shade's dream.
I am the earth, you are the sky,
I am the picture; you are the memories that never die.

I am the journey, you are the destination,
   I am the drive; you are the inspiration.
   Your eyes make my heart race,
   In them, I find my place.

If I am troubled, you are my relief,
If I am lost, you are my belief.
If life fades, you are my light above,
Your presence, my eternal love.

Your eyes keep me alive when

all seems lost,
   In your gaze, my worries are tossed.
   Without you, I'd wander alone and cold,
   But with you, my story is beautifully told.
   In you, I've found my guardian, my grace,
   In every challenge, I see your face.

So here I stand, my heart in view,
Kara, my love, forever to you."

The audience, including Kara, is captivated by Kevin's heartfelt words. Upon hearing this, Kara's heart fills with love, and everyone around is shocked. They all look at Kara, whose face turns red with embarrassment. David starts dancing in joy, and Bella also becomes happy. All the girls are smitten by Kevin's poem, becoming Kevin's admirers. Everyone chants Kara and Kevin's names loudly. Even the professors applaud Kevin's achievement, comparing him to William Shakespeare of this generation. Kara remains very happy and keeps looking at Kevin. Kevin comes down from the stage and kneels on one knee, offering a rose to Kara. Kara accepts it without hesitation, overwhelmed with happiness.

Revelations and Confrontations

Alex, witnessing everything unfold, realizes his entire scheme has crumbles. He seizes Kara's hand in front of everyone, pulls her aside, and slaps her. He confronts her angrily, "What have you done? You never even thought about me. You've made a mistake, and now I'm going to call my dad and tell him everything." Undeterred, Kara responds defiantly, "I'm not afraid anymore. I now have the courage to confess my love for Kevin. If not you, then him." Upon hearing this, Alex proceeds to call his father and explain everything.

As everything unfolds, Alex's father immediately fires Kara's father from his job, saying, "Your daughter betrayed my son by choosing a poor man like Kevin over him. "What did Kevin have that your daughter gave him so much importance? You are worthless too.". When Kara's father gets very angry, Kara's father never think that their daughter will do so. Then he give Kara the last warning and say that if you left Alex, I would kill Kevin, do you want Kevin stays alive? Kara starts crying when she hears this.

"Dad, I love Kevin. Please don't harm Kevin. I will do as you told me."

She accepts her father's words, knowing he has the power to harm Kevin. Kara goes to Alex with Kevin and apologizes, 'Forgive me, Kevin. I cannot betray Alex. He never meant any harm. Alex is a good person.' Hearing this, Kevin is saddened. You did not do right. If you had to do this, why did you accept my love, my love, in front of everyone? When Kara lies that I did not want to humiliate you in college, again, I want your last year to go well, inside her mind she is saying all this hurts my heart, but I still have to say it so that Your life could be saved my love.

Kevin's Heartbreak

Kevin feels very hurt after hearing Kara's words. He runs away from there, not looking back, and runs very far away, not even looking at Kara's face. He runs far away, then sits under a tree near the sea shore of the college, where he always goes when he is sad. There, David and Bella come again to Kevin to understand him, and they are accompanied by Ben and Lily to understand Kevin.

David reassures, "Kara is speaking out of fear of her father. Don't worry, Kevin. She truly loves you. I overheard Kara speaking to her father from behind. It seems her father said something to her, and when Kara cried and said, 'I will do as you say,' perhaps that's why she chose to be with Alex. Don't take Kara's words to heart. We all saw how she accepted your rose in front of everyone; there was love in her eyes for you, tears. By saying this David had convinced him.

The Dark Plan: Alex's Final Option

Seeing Kara's love for Kevin, Alex believes his only option left is to ensure Kevin's death to win Kara. Alex and his father collaborate to plan Kevin's demise with the help of researcher, a friend of Alex's father who owns a research centre in Frank wood Village. The centre which was sealed by the government years ago, holds significance. Alex's father insists that Alex cannot take Kevin alone there. Instead, he suggests gathering all seven friends for a trip to Frank wood's forests, disguised as a celebration for their final year of college and also to find idea for their final year project. After convincing Kara first and then Ben, everyone eventually agrees. final year of college, but Kevin not agrees with that but he is also convinced by the Kara.

Into the Darkness

After completing all preparations, everyone gathers and boards Alex's large car, heading towards Frank wood Village. Alex drives through the night, arriving in Frank wood Village and proceeding from there into the dense jungle where the research centre is located. It is a dark night, with everyone else asleep in the car as Alex drives slowly into the forest. As they approach, Alex notices that the forest has been sealed off with a gate and locked.

Alex, determined, somehow manages to break the lock on the gate after getting out of the car and quietly approaching it. Finding the lock sturdy, Alex comes up with an idea: he uses his lighter, which he had secretly brought along, to set fire to a cloth soaked in diesel that he pulls out of the car and ignites it. In the midst of this, Ben wakes up and notices Alex outside the car, wondering what he's doing. Seeing the locked gate, Alex tells Ben that he lost the key and is burning it for some reason, and convinces Ben. Together, they burn the chain and, after it melts, remove it to open the gate and drive the car inside, closing the gate behind them to avoid suspicion.

The Arrival at the Research Centre

After arriving at the research centre around 2 AM, and Alex sees the broken door of the research centre. Now he wakes everyone up in the car, and they all look out. It was very late at night and very dark, and nobody could see anything. No one knew that it was a research centre. Kevin tells everyone, "Let's go inside, this is my farmhouse, we'll be staying here." Saying this, he leads everyone into the research centre, with Alex following. The research centre appears heavily damaged, with broken windows and an odd smell lingering in the air. Alex takes his friends to the guest room and they rest there for now. After everyone falls asleep, deeply exhausted, Alex steps out of the guest room and calls his father. In a hushed voice, he says, "The job is done as you instructed." His father replies, "Now go to sleep. Tomorrow I'll send some goons to kill Kevin." Alex hangs up the call. As Alex walks back to the guest room, he hears a noise that sounds like an animal snoring. Thinking it's just his imagination, he dismisses the sound and goes back to the guest room, where he falls asleep.

Discovery at the Research Centre

The next day, Lily wakes up first and, looking outside, she screams in shock. Everyone rushes out and is shocked to see a dead lion with half its body eaten, blood stains scattered around.

Furious, everyone confronts Alex, demanding to know where he has taken them and what place he has brought them to. Kevin notices a laboratory with the sign "Research Centre" above the door, shocking everyone into investigating further. And he says, "This is the same research centre that was sealed by the government due to illegal research without permission."

And David also supports Kevin, saying, "Yes, that's right. I remember reading in the news that they were researching some mysterious egg here without government permission, which is why it was sealed. Alex, why did you bring us all here?"

Kara gets very angry at Alex, and Alex tries to save himself by lying, "I didn't know this was a research centre. My father made me believe it was my old farmhouse. I couldn't see in the darkness like you guys could. Please forgive me," he says as he tries to save himself.

When David tells Alex that they need to leave this place quickly because staying at his supposed farmhouse here seems dangerous, Alex apologizes, "Sorry, guys, we can't leave. The car is out of fuel." and also here the phone network signal is also weak, but don't worry. Last night, there was some network signal, so I called my dad and asked him to send fuel.

The Haunting Call of the Wild

Upon hearing what Alex said, everyone checks their phone signals outside. A terrifying animalistic sound grows louder. David and Ben rush inside, urging everyone to hide as an animal approaches. And as they run, they spot stairs leading down to the basement. They descend the stairs, and Alex keeps saying, "Don't run, I'm here. Why fear? Let's talk about our bravery." He thinks, "Maybe Dad sent goons. They might be making noises."

And as everyone begins to hide in the basement, they come across a broken door leading to a secret lab. Inside, they see a shattered egg. Kara exclaims, "Look there! Is that the same broken egg they were researching?" Kevin agrees, "Yes, Kara. It seems like that egg." Perhaps the creature from that egg has emerged outside. That could be its sound. Alex quickly interjects, "Kevin, don't say anything! If it hears us, we're in trouble. How could it be possible?"

Just then, they hear voices outside, possibly people coming to rescue them. Understanding it as a chance to escape, everyone quickly leaves the basement and exits the area.

Only Kara remains in the basement, where she suddenly gets phone signal. At that moment, she receives a message from her police officer uncle. Meanwhile, everyone else—David, Ben, Kevin, Bella, and Lily—comes outside and sees armed goons. Alex tries to signal and indicate that Kevin is the one, repeating "Kevin, it's him!" but they don't understand at first. One of the goon asserts, "You're Alex, right? Your dad sent me to take care of a guy named Kevin. Which one of these is Kevin?" They all glare at Alex, awaiting his response.

The Truth Unveiled

continues talking to her uncle, who explains, "Stay away from Alex. Everything that has happened to you so far, he's behind it all. We've figured it out. Alex is a bad guy." Alex was the one who pushed Kevin towards you in the college canteen, placed the papers in Kevin's bag, and threw a stone at Kevin's head. And he had intentionally collided with your mom's car so that you couldn't reach Kevin in the hospital. Kevin is innocent. Alex wants money from you. Alex and his father want to take your property. They both made this plan together. "It was discovered that Alex's father recommended to killers to kill the Kevin, and you have to save Kevin".

Kara felt remorse for his actions. The police officer also kept writing that he informed everything to your father, and now father also supports Kara."

"When Kara replies to the message, she calls for help from Frankwood's sealed research centre. Just as she is about to send another message, the signal suddenly goes out. Kara becomes very nervous. After all the truth comes out in front of Alex, she understands everything. Now she realizes that Alex is the biggest threat."

"I feel very bad about what I did with Kevin. I hurt Kevin a lot by saying that. He gets emotional and at other times, there are arguments between Alex and the David. At that time, Kara comes outside and says that Alex did all this. Alex called everyone there. Alex deceived us all, "Alex is a coward and a traitor. He came here to kill Kevin. Alex intentionally lied to us and brought us here to kill Kevin. Then Alex says, 'Yes, this is all my plan. Now you're too late, Kara. You can't save your Kevin anymore.'"

Kara's Plea

"Now you all will die with Kevin," then Kara says, "Kevin, run from here. Kevin, don't worry about me; they will kill you. Tears in her eyes, saying something like this:

"You are my life, please run from here,
By my love, I beg you, disappear.
I'd rather die than see you in pain,
Go now, my love, before it's in vain."

But Kevin doesn't leave, and just then something inside comes in. Everyone, David, Kevin, Bella, and all their friends, look towards the direction of the goons and keep staring. When the goons shout loudly, 'What happened, scared to see us?' That's when Alex says, 'Look behind you.' When they slowly look behind, the goons.

They see a 6-foot tall Spinosaurus who continuously emits liquid from its mouth, appearing very fierce and hungry. The dinosaur attacks the goons directly, causing everyone there to flee. Upon seeing the

Spinosaurus, David, Bella, Ben, Lily, and then Alex and Kevin look at it. But when Kara starts to run away, her foot gets stuck in a pit below.

At that moment, Kevin looks back at Kara and returns to her. He pulls Kara's foot out of the pit and holds her hand to run away, but none of their friends are visible around them. But by then, the Spinosaurus has already attacked and defeated all the goons. It then turns towards Kara and Kevin.

A Flight Through Blossoms

Kevin grabs Kara's hand and they start running together, amidst the chaotic aftermath of the Spinosaurus attacking the goons.

When he takes her hand and they start to flee,
It feels like joy showers endlessly.
Through thorny paths, trees cast their leaves,

Flowers carpet their
way, in fragrant reprieve.
The blossoms perfume the air with delight,
Protecting their steps, making everything right.
Together they run, like a star with the moon,
Or a comet racing, as wishes attune.
Their bond shines brightly, a celestial sight,
Like a star and moon, in the daylight.
As they run, they colour the world anew,
Turning shadows into a vibrant view.

As they run swiftly, Kara keeps looking back at Kevin, her hand tightly gripping his, joyfully fleeing together. When Kevin finally mentions the Spinosaurus, Kara recalls reading about it in a childhood encyclopaedia:

"The Spinosaurus is a well-known dinosaur described as a carnivore capable of surviving on both land and in water. It was among the largest carnivorous dinosaurs, distinguished by its sail-like structure on its back. Adaptations such as dense bones for buoyancy, conical teeth for catching fish, and paddle-like limbs for swimming suggest it was adept in aquatic environments. It hunted terrestrial prey and aquatic animals, making it a formidable predator."

Their escape continues, finding refuge wherever they can, their hearts racing with each step as they navigate the perils around them.

When Kara says that we might weaken it by attacking its weak parts, but before that, we have to find the rest of the friends when the Spinosaurus goes away.

Kevin's Promise

Kevin stops Kara from coming with him upon realizing that the Spinosaurus is in the opposite direction and it's risky to take her there. He says to her, "You stay here, I'll go search for the others." He halts her and heads off to find their friends, successfully locating them and returning to Kara's side. He goes to search for the other friends, finds them, and returns to Kara's location. When Kara is about to come to Kevin, Alex sees the Spinosaurus moving away from Kara towards another direction.

Now, Alex should not have Kara or Kevin, so Alex shouts loudly and runs away from there Then, as the Spinosaurus runs towards Kara, Kevin also runs towards her to save her. Just then, David finds a knife nearby and throws it towards Kevin, saying "Take this, Kevin!"

Then, Kevin grabs the knife and attacks the Spinosaurus's weak spot, the sail on its back, in front of Kara, saving her. But the Spinosaurus's claws hit Kevin's head, were operation had taken place last year

The Brave Sacrifice

After the knife stabbing the Spinosaurus, it dies, and due to the Spinosaurus' nails stabbing Kevin's head As Kevin starts bleeding profusely from his head due to the Spinosaurus' claw piercing, Kara catches him as he begins to fall. Kara's body becomes covered in Kevin's blood.

Kara now sits down, taking Kevin in her lap, and starts crying a lot. Kevin, nothing will happen to you, nothing will happen to you. Keep courage, you have to stay alive for me She cries, saying, "You won't die, Kevin," and hugs him tightly, taking a piece of her clothing and wrapping it around his head

But a lot of time passes and a lot of blood has flowed, there is no hospital nearby. Now, there was no chance for Kevin to survive, now Kevin looks at Kara

In her arms, facing death's embrace,

He whispers, "No regrets, for with you, life's grace.

Gazing at you, it feels like heaven's call,

Better to die here than live without you at all."

Saying this, Kevin smiles and closes his eyes as he looks at Kara. When Kara cries out in anguish, Kevin's words make her cry heavily.

Witnessing her love lying lifeless, she weeps,
Like a crane mourning its mate, softly she speaks.
"You can't leave me, not now," she cries,
Even the sun sets at Kevin's sight, Kara sighs.

Memories linger, in whispers of the past,
A love too deep, too fleeting to last.
With every tear shed, a piece of her heart,
Fades into silence, as they drift apart.

Unbearable Loss

Now David sits down below, crying. He has lost his best friend, and tears come to Bella's eyes as well. Saying that I have lost a brother-like friend, even Ben and Lily become sad

Now at that time, Alex tries to escape in his car after attempting to kill Kevin. Just then, Kara's police uncle arrives with the police, arrests Alex, and takes him inside. When they see Kevin lying dead in Kara's lap, everyone, including the police officers, take off their caps. Kara faints while crying, and her uncle takes her to his car and comforts her. They call an ambulance for Kevin's body and take it home.

Kevin's parents cannot bear this anymore; they have lost their other son too. Now, they cannot bear it

Now at the funeral ,they bury Kevin in the cemetery, and David, Bella, and all of Kevin's friends are there. Kara still keeps crying

And the next day, Kevin's parents leave the city, leaving everything behind, without anyone knowing. They had no reason to live anymore after losing their son, so they leave everything behind

Kara's father now apologizes to Kara for his behaviour, and the truth about Alex and his father comes out. They are sentenced to life imprisonment for their actions.

Forever in Memory

Kara now lives relying on memories of Kevin. Sometimes she cries, and sometimes she smiles, remembering how badly she treated Kevin, yet he saved her. Many years pass, and Kara still lives in the memories of Kevin. She writes her love for Kevin in a way as

"Eternal Remembrance"
Years have passed, yet Kevin's memory stays,
Kara remains in sorrow, through all her days.
Recalling every harsh word said,
She weeps for the love she once had.

Gazing at the sky, her heart begins to cry,

"You left like the wind, gone high and dry.

Forgive me, dear, for every regret,

**I am your Juliet,
you're my Romeo.**

"I am your Rose, you are my Jack,
Lost to the depths, no turning back.
You drifted away like water's flow,
Forgotten me, like a tale long ago.

"I remember, and wait for you still,
Living this life, against my will.
You saved me once, so here I remain,
Searching for you, through joy and pain

"I find you only in one place, my heart,

Wishing to see, hear, and feel every part.
God's cruel, keeping us apart,
Not letting me reach where you are.
"Wait for me in heaven, my dear,
I'll come to you, never fear.
Love me always, as You do,
In heaven's embrace, our love renews."

As the sun sets, the moon rises; as light fades, darkness ascends. Yet beyond this life, in heaven, they shall reunite, where eternal love transcends even death.

———-Written and Design by M. Kaif

Embark on a chilling journey as secrets unfold within the darkened halls of the cursed palace, where each step reverberates with whispers of forgotten horrors and mysteries waiting to be unearthed.

The Cursed Palace - Chapter 1

Now available on Amazon.